Peppa Pig™

Miss Rabbit's Day Off

Peppa, George and Suzy Sheep have had a
sleepover at Rebecca Rabbit's house.

Crunch!

Munch!

Crunch!

"It's fun having carrots for breakfast!" laughs Peppa.
"I could eat carrots all day!" agrees Daddy Rabbit.

Mummy Rabbit's sister, Miss Rabbit, pops in to say hello.

"I can't stop long," she says. "I've got lots of work to do. I'm working at the supermarket, selling ice creams and driving the bus!"

Miss Rabbit trips over
one of Richard's toys.
Her ankle is hurt.

"You must stay here and get better," decides Mummy Rabbit. "I'll do your work for you."

Oww!

Mummy Rabbit puts
Rebecca and her friends
in charge of looking
after Miss Rabbit.

Luckily, Suzy Sheep has her
nurse's outfit with her.

"Don't worry," she says.
"I am only a
pretend nurse!"

Peppa phones Miss Rabbit's
ice cream stall.
Daddy Pig answers.
"Miss Rabbit is ill.
You've got to sell the
ice cream today!"
"Ho, ho!" snorts
Daddy Pig. "I'm an
expert at ice cream!"
He gets to work.

Selling ice cream is quite hard.
Soon the ice cream begins to melt.

The ice cream is all runny.
"Ice cream soup anyone?" asks Daddy Pig.

Peppa phones Grandad Dog.
"Miss Rabbit is very ill. Can you
drive her bus today please?"

Grandad Dog gets to work, but driving a bus is quite hard. It is even harder when you have cars to fix, too.

Back at Rebecca Rabbit's
house, Miss Rabbit is
feeling better.
"Can I get up now?"
she asks.

Suzy Sheep shakes her head. "No! You must lie very still . . . but please keep breathing."

"It's not easy doing all your jobs," says Mummy Rabbit at the end of the day. "It's not easy sitting down all day!" says Miss Rabbit. She will definitely be back at work tomorrow!